Food as Foe

Nutrition and Eating Disorders

Lesli J. Favor
with Kira Freed

Marshall Cavendish
Benchmark
New York

Marshall Cavendish Benchmark
99 White Plains Road
Tarrytown, NY 10591
www.marshallcavendish.us

Library of Congress Cataloging-in-Publication Data

Favor, Lesli J.
    Food as foe : nutrition and eating disorders / by Lesli J. Favor with Kira Freed.
      p. cm. — (Benchmark rockets. Food and you)
    Includes index.
    Summary: "An introduction to nutrition and eating disorders. Discusses
information about eating disorders and ways to develop a healthy relationship
with food"—Provided by publisher.
    ISBN 978-0-7614-4364-3
  1. Eating disorders—Juvenile literature. 2. Children—Nutrition—Juvenile
literature. I. Freed, Kira. II. Title.

RC552.E18F382 2010
618.92'8526—dc22
2008054284

Publisher: Michelle Bisson
Editorial Development and Book Design: Trillium Publishing, Inc.

Photo research by Trillium Publishing, Inc.

Cover photo: Shutterstock.com/Elena Ray

The photographs and illustrations in this book are used by permission and
through the courtesy of: iStockphoto.com: Diego Alvarez de Toledo, 1; Mathieu
Viennet, 3; Kathleen & Scott Snowden, 4; vm, 20. Shutterstock.com: Losevsky
Pavel, 5; Sonja Foos, 9; Morgan Lane Photography, 22. PhotoEdit: Spencer Grant,
7; David Kelly Crow, 17. Corbis: Keith Bedford/Reuters/Corbis, 19. USDA: 25.

Printed in Malaysia
1 3 5 6 4 2

Contents

1 Food: Friend or Foe?

Selena kneels on the floor of her friend's bathroom, vomiting into the toilet. She hopes the music from Eva's radio covers the sounds. None of the girls at Eva's sleepover know that Selena **purges** *after she eats foods like the pizza they shared. She makes up for eating in public by starving herself at home. Selena feels tired all the time. On some days, it takes all of her focus just to perform basic tasks.*

Selena has an eating disorder. She may feel painfully alone in her situation, but she is not. Millions of Americans suffer from eating disorders. About one in every hundred teenage Americans is affected.

*Joshua frowns as he completes his twelfth repetition with the heavy barbell. After his upper body workout, he will start on his lower body. Dinner can wait. In fact, he will skip dinner tonight. He is only thinking about how to add another inch to his chest and lose another inch from his waist. Joshua already works out seven days a week and he plans to add two more weekend workouts. He also plans to cut out another hundred **calories** a day. He tells himself that feeling hungry proves that he is losing body fat and making his muscles stand out more each day.*

Joshua has an eating disorder, too. Like other males with eating disorders, he is torn between trying to enlarge his muscles and trying to get rid of every bit of body fat. Most of his thoughts focus on these two goals. Fewer males than females have eating disorders, but the number of males with these disorders is growing.

What exactly is an eating disorder? Two experts on eating disorders, Christopher G. Fairburn

Feeling pressure to achieve a particular body type can lead to an eating disorder.

and B. Timothy Walsh, give this definition: an eating disorder is "a persistent disturbance of eating behavior or behavior intended to control weight, which significantly impairs physical health or psychosocial functioning."

Someone with an eating disorder may severely cut back on food intake or eat large amounts of food. He or she may purge food from the body or exercise **compulsively** to stay trim. Or the person might eat huge amounts of food and carry extra weight. In any of these cases, the person's **nutritional** balance suffers, and his or her health risks increase. In some cases, the result is death.

We eat to stay alive and to nourish our bodies. It's that simple—or is it? Even if we don't realize it, we also eat for many other reasons. We eat to fuel—or fight—emotions. We eat because those around us are eating. We also eat—or refuse to eat—because of messages and images from the media, our families, and our social groups. And we eat as a response to our own body images.

This book offers information to help you understand eating disorders—the main types, risks, treatments, and causes. Eating disorders are serious health threats. Reliable information can help you recognize symptoms early and address the causes. Young people who may already have an eating disorder can learn the importance of getting **professional** help.

As people with eating disorders begin to recover, they are able to give more attention to healthy ways of eating. They can build a healthy relationship with food. Let's begin by exploring patterns of eating.

Myth: A thin person is a healthy person.

Fact: A thin person with poor eating and exercise habits can be just as unhealthy as an overweight person with poor eating and exercise habits.

2 Healthy and Unhealthy Patterns of Eating

We get many mixed messages about food. As children we are taught that food helps us grow big and strong. As we get older and make our own food choices, we learn that some foods are more healthful than others. Each day involves many food choices. We decide when, what, and how much to eat. All these choices can become **overwhelming**.

What does healthy eating really mean? There is no single right way to organize daily meals and snacks. It is normal to change the foods you eat, and when you eat, from day to day. These changes can be part of healthy eating. Understanding healthy and unhealthy patterns of eating over time is more important than sticking to a strict meal plan.

Imagine a young woman, Ana, who follows a pattern of eating healthily when hungry, stopping when full, and getting some exercise most days. Ana will stay at about the same weight, perhaps going up or down 5 to 10 pounds.

A healthy pattern of eating creates a balance between energy taken in through food and energy the body uses. We use calories to measure the energy in food. Ana eats the number of calories her body needs to carry out its normal daily functions. Those calories include a healthy selection of foods rather than just fast or junk foods. Now compare Ana's eating and exercise patterns with the unhealthy patterns listed in "Warning Signs of an Eating Disorder."

The National Eating Disorders Association estimates that between 5 and 10 million Americans have an eating disorder. Eating disorders occur in children, **adolescents**, and

Warning Signs of an Eating Disorder

Food behaviors: regularly skipping meals or eating only tiny amounts; regular excuses for not eating; only eating low-calorie foods; hiding or throwing away food; purging food to keep from gaining weight.

Body image behaviors: insisting that he or she is fat when this is not true; disgusted by body size or shape; wearing clothes that hide a bony body.

Exercise behaviors: compulsively exercising, even to the point of exhaustion.

Thoughts and emotions: believing that being thin will bring happiness, love, or another emotional benefit; believing that thin people are happier or more successful than those with average bodies; denying an eating problem; envying thinner people; feeling guilty, unworthy, hopeless, powerless, or unloved.

adults of both sexes. They occur in all social classes and races. Most eating disorders develop in young people aged 12 to 18. But they have been reported in younger children and in adults in their 70s. Most of these people are female, but 10 percent or more are males.

Anorexia Nervosa

Anorexia nervosa, or anorexia, is a medical condition in which the most obvious symptom is extremely low body weight. People with anorexia are **obsessed** with being thin. They see themselves as fat when, in fact, they are extremely thin. Anorexic people spend a great deal of effort avoiding food. They also stay away from situations in which they are expected to eat. They find ways to avoid eating and to hide food that others think they have eaten. They make excuses for why they are not eating. When they do eat or drink, they choose very low-calorie items, such as celery and diet drinks. Eating can feel disgusting or frightening to people with anorexia. Some force themselves to throw up the food they eat. Others may exercise for long periods of time to burn off calories. These behaviors cause the person's body weight to fall dangerously low and lead to a loss of muscle.

Even though they appear thin to others, people with anorexia believe they are overweight.

Anorexia most often occurs in teenage girls, but boys may also develop the disorder. Females usually focus on becoming as thin as possible. Males often starve themselves while trying to build muscle and look athletic.

Anorexia might seem to be about looks. But, like other eating disorders, it is a medical illness that usually results from trying to use food and body weight to control other problems. Anorexia causes a person's physical, mental, and emotional health to suffer. The person may not be aware of the problems that are causing the illness.

Anorexia can destroy a person's health and should always be treated as a serious medical concern. Between 5 and 19 percent of people with anorexia die because of the health problems that result from starving themselves. Among those with anorexia whose disease has not been treated, the death rate is closer to 25 percent.

Some Physical Symptoms of Anorexia Nervosa

- Body weight that is about 20 percent below normal.

- Soft, fluffy hair on the face and arms.

- Dry, scaly skin.

- Fainting or feeling light-headed.

- Frequent scratches or cuts on knuckles (from forced vomiting).

- In females, irregular periods or no periods.

People who have anorexia face serious medical problems. These include **malnutrition** and a slowing down of the basic body functions that require body fat as fuel. These body functions include blood pressure and breathing. Not eating enough can also damage the heart, liver, and kidneys. Other problems include swollen joints, brittle bones, and anemia. Anemia is too low a level of red blood cells, which are needed to carry oxygen throughout the body. A girl whose periods stop (or never begin in the first place) because of anorexia can have weakened bones and other long-term health problems.

Anorexia can be treated. The person sees a team of health-care professionals, including those who treat both the physical and mental/emotional issues. Treatment includes gaining weight as well as learning about nutrition and exercise. **Psychotherapy** helps patients discover and deal with the problems that contribute to their anorexia. Therapy also helps patients change long-held, harmful ideas about weight, body size, **self-image**, and self-confidence. Medicine for **depression**, **anxiety**, or other emotional conditions may be needed. Sometimes a hospital stay will be needed. If not, regular appointments with health-care professionals are a necessity.

Treatment takes time and patience. **Relapses** are common. According to the American Academy of Pediatrics, about one-third of patients "have long-term problems coping with food and accepting a normal weight." The chances of survival and recovery are better if a patient gets treatment early.

Bulimia Nervosa

Bulimia nervosa, or bulimia, is an eating disorder that involves cycles of **binging** and purging. The person **gorges**, or eats a huge amount of food at one time, to the point of causing the stomach to hurt. Then he or she forces the food out of the body. Like people with anorexia, people with bulimia obsess about food, body size, and body weight. Their self-worth and body image are tied to how thin they see themselves as being. Unlike people with anorexia, people with bulimia usually have a body weight that is close to normal for their height. Their body size may appear a little thin, a little plump, or average. About 80 percent of people with bulimia binge and then use some method to purge the food. The other 20 percent binge but do not purge. People in either group may **fast** and exercise too much to make up for their binging.

This **urge** to gorge is not a response to hunger. Instead, it is caused by feelings of anxiety, tension, powerlessness, or other emotions. On average, a person with bulimia binges at least once a day and often more. When the urge to gorge fades away, strong feelings of guilt, shame, depression, disgust, sadness, or frustration set in. The person's stomach may become stretched out from the large amounts of food it contains, and the stomach may ache.

These painful emotional and physical responses cause a very strong urge to get rid of the food that was eaten. Forced vomiting and the use of products to empty solid and liquid wastes from the body are common choices. Some people with bulimia develop a strict exercise routine, and some turn to drugs. Others starve themselves for long periods to make up for binging.

Bulimia occurs mainly in females. The disorder usually develops in girls during their late teens or early twenties. It can occur in younger teens as well. It is hard to know how many people are affected since most people with bulimia hide their binging and purging.

Even though people with bulimia may have a normal body weight, their bodies are not necessarily healthy. Binging and purging cause serious and sometimes permanent damage—sometimes even death.

Vomiting causes fluids from the stomach to come up into the mouth. This can cause serious dental problems. Frequent vomiting can also harm the tube between the throat and stomach, which can be life-threatening. Frequent vomiting can also damage the stomach, heart, lungs, and kidneys.

Some Physical Symptoms of Bulimia Nervosa

- Frequent scratches or cuts on knuckles (from forced vomiting).
- Damaged enamel on teeth (from stomach acid).
- Swollen glands in the neck and face.
- Stomach pain.
- Sore throat.
- Ongoing problem with heartburn.

Like other eating disorders, bulimia can be treated. The main goal of treatment is to help people with bulimia separate body-image issues from the other conflicts in their lives. They must learn not to blame their appearance for their problems.

Psychological therapy and nutritional education are both important in the treatment of bulimia. A mental health professional can help a person with bulimia understand and address the causes of eating disorders. A nutritional expert can teach healthy patterns of eating. Over time, patients learn to solve their problems and cope with difficult situations without turning to food. In most cases, people with bulimia can be treated outside of a hospital.

Ten years after being **diagnosed**, about 70 percent of people with bulimia are much better. About 20 percent are somewhat better. About 10 percent have completely returned to binging and purging. Fewer than one percent will die as a result of bulimia.

Binge-Eating Disorder

Binge eating involves the frequent eating of huge amounts of food when not hungry. Unlike a person with bulimia, the binge eater does not purge the food or use exercise to make up for gorging. As a result, most people with this disorder are overweight or **obese**. Binge-eating disorder may begin in early childhood, but most patients are middle-aged. More females than males have this disorder.

People who suffer from binge-eating disorder are at risk for health problems related to obesity. The most common cause of death in the United States is heart disease, which is directly related to extra body fat and body weight. Obese men and women are also at greater risk for many other serious conditions, including some cancers. People with serious weight issues are also more likely to suffer physical pain and feel worse in general.

Low self-esteem is common in binge eaters. They may have poor skills in social settings. Activities with friends, classmates, or other people can seem like too much trouble. These situations can cause the binge eater to have feelings of failure, depression, or anxiety. Like other people with eating disorders, binge eaters may try to stay away from social settings, especially those involving food.

Some Symptoms of Binge-Eating Disorder

- Repeated episodes of binge eating—usually two or more days a week for six months or longer.
- Feeling a lack of control over eating or feeling unable to stop eating.
- Eating much faster than normal during the binge, often too quickly to taste the food.
- Eating huge amounts of food when not hungry.
- Eating alone to hide the amount of food being eaten.
- Feelings of guilt, shame, or disgust following the binge.
- Being overweight or obese.

Researchers see a connection between dieting and the start of binge-eating patterns. Dieting keeps people from feeling full after a good meal. Real hunger and the lack of fullness can bring on a binge eater's urge to gorge. But, as with other eating disorders, eating in response to painful emotions is also a large factor.

Binge eating, like anorexia and bulimia, requires medical and psychological treatment. Therapy can help binge eaters explore the causes of the painful emotions that fuel their urge to gorge. A main goal of treatment is to teach patients how to eat in response to hunger, not feelings. Patients learn to eat and exercise in amounts that keep them at a healthy weight for their height. A nutritionist may teach patients how to choose a variety of healthful foods with a treat of sweets or fast food once in a while. Regular, planned mealtimes and snacks help establish healthy eating behaviors. Eating at regular times teaches the body to know when it is time to eat. As a result, hunger lets patients know when to eat. Fullness becomes a sign to stop eating.

As with any eating disorder, there are no quick solutions to binge-eating disorder. Professional treatment helps patients understand the disorder, address the causes, and make the needed changes to their lifestyles.

3
Eating Disorders: Causes and Solutions

Many people mistakenly believe that eating disorders are caused by the lack of **willpower** or the lack of knowledge about nutrition, or both. The truth is that eating disorders are usually about much more than food. Understanding the real causes of eating disorders is necessary for treatment and recovery.

People with eating disorders often use patterns of eating as a way to manage overwhelming emotions. They may overeat to "stuff down" feelings they can't handle. They may starve themselves to feel powerful in one area of their lives. They may purge food to try to get rid of painful emotions. Eating disorders may also be a response to social pressures to match a certain image. The following factors can all play a role in the development of eating disorders.

Painful emotions: Many situations can cause painful emotions. These emotions may include depression, loneliness, anger, and anxiety. If a person does not learn healthy ways to express and heal painful emotions, the emotions remain. The person may lose hope of healing. Food may come to replace the real comfort and nourishment a person needs.

Difficult situations: Distressing situations in our daily lives often contribute to eating disorders. These situations may involve troubled relationships with family or friends. They may also include being teased or shamed for one's weight or size, or having a history of physical or sexual abuse. A fire, a car accident, a medical problem, or the loss of a loved one can leave a person feeling overwhelmed.

Family history: If family members have, or have had, eating disorders, children may be more likely to develop them as well. A family history of depression or other mental illness can also be a factor. If a parent focuses too much on appearance and thinness, children receive unhealthy messages about what is important in life. Conflicts between family members, a lack of emotional support, and other unhealthy family patterns can influence the development of an eating disorder. Caregivers who use food to reward or punish can cause food to represent much more than nourishment for the body.

Self-image: Your self-image is how you judge your own worth. Self-image includes how you think about both your inner self—your thoughts and feelings—and your outer self—your physical body. Self-image is influenced by culture and society. It is also influenced by how you compare yourself to the **ideals** around you. Every day, we see many images of super-thin female movie stars and well-muscled males. These images remind us of our culture's focus on appearance over inner qualities. Social pressures to fit in and follow the crowd strengthen these messages. If you don't think you measure up, your self-esteem and body image can suffer. This can spark painful emotions and contribute to an unhealthy relationship with food.

Other factors: There may also be other factors that play a role in the development of eating disorders. Researchers are exploring possible chemical, biological, and **inherited** factors.

The fashion industry promotes the idea that what's on the outside is all that matters.

Because of all these different factors, no one can point to a certain risk factor or type of person and say for sure whether someone is likely to develop an eating disorder. Each person responds to pressures and emotions in his or her own way. Each person's journey to healing is individual as well.

It is a myth that recovery from eating disorders requires only nutritional education and wiser food choices. The complex set of factors that contribute to eating disorders requires a complex set of solutions. You may suffer from an eating disorder, have friends who do, or want to do your best to avoid having one in the future. In all cases, a program of self-care can be your best protection. So what can help?

- Spend time getting to know your inner self—your strengths, your likes and dislikes, and who you are becoming as a person.

- Everyone struggles with painful emotions from time to time. Identify the causes of your suffering as a first step toward finding solutions. Have an honest talk with yourself about what's "eating" you and what you might be "stuffing." The support of a good friend can help you feel safer to explore areas of concern.

- Consider seeing a therapist if you aren't getting support in your everyday life. A good therapist can help you sort through your beliefs and develop healthier ones to replace the ones that do not serve you. A therapist can also help you learn better ways to resolve painful emotions.

Professionals who specialize in eating disorders understand the challenges their patients face.

- If something troubling is happening in your life, get help. Talk with a teacher, therapist, or another trusted adult. If the problem is physical or sexual abuse, contact an abuse hotline or Child Protective Services.
- Give yourself the support you need to develop a healthy body image. Remember that you, like the people around you, have grown up in a culture that values image more than a person's true worth. Take a break from television, films, and magazines. Spend more time with real people.
- Choose friends who value you as you are. Amazing people come in all shapes and sizes. You don't have to look or act like anyone else to be worthy, lovable, attractive, or productive.
- Get rid of the bathroom scale. Think about your body based on how you feel and how you take care of yourself, not by how much you weigh.
- Give your body the nutrition, exercise, and rest it needs to be healthy. If you can't do this right now, then accept yourself wherever you are on your healing journey. Seek out people who support your faith in the future.

"We as women are trained to see ourselves as cheap imitations of fashion photographs, rather than seeing fashion photographs as cheap imitations of women . . ."
—Naomi Wolf, *The Beauty Myth*

4 Food and Wellness

Nutritious food is necessary for physical growth during **puberty** and adolescence. A young person's body grows and develops quickly during this time. This is also when many young people begin to take charge of their own food choices and eating habits. Yet they may know little about the serving sizes and kinds of foods that their bodies need to stay healthy.

People who suffer from eating disorders often cannot focus on learning how to eat well. Instead, their focus is on the issues that cause their eating disorder. As the causes of their eating disorder are resolved, they can pay more attention to learning to eat healthily.

The Six Classes of Nutrients

The body needs six classes of nutrients to survive: proteins, fats, carbohydrates, vitamins, minerals, and water.

Proteins are needed for the growth and repair of tissues such as muscle, bone, **cartilage**, and teeth. The building blocks of protein help control body functions such as carrying oxygen to cells and fighting infection. High-protein foods include eggs, milk, meat, fish, and poultry, as well as some vegetables, grains, and beans. In general, low-fat protein sources are more healthful than high-fat sources.

Fats may come from animals or plants. Fats are a good source of energy. The body also needs fats for healthy cells, **blood clotting**, and other functions.

All Fats Are Not Created Equal

As a general rule, healthier fats are liquid at room temperature. Unhealthier fats are solid at room temperature.

- **Healthier fats:** Fats that are considered healthier are found in olive, canola, vegetable, and nut oils; avocados; nuts; and cold-water fish, such as salmon.

- **Unhealthier fats:** Fats that are less healthy are found in red meats, dairy products, and tropical oils. These fats are best eaten in limited amounts.

- **Trans fats:** These fats are linked to many health problems and should be avoided. Trans fats are found in most margarines, shortenings, and in foods that contain these products, such as cookies and crackers.

Carbohydrates include sugars, starches, and most fibers. Foods rich in carbohydrates include cereals, grains, fruits, vegetables, pasta, potatoes, and sugary foods and drinks. Most carbohydrates, the sugars and starches, are **converted** into **glucose**. Glucose is an energy source for the body. Most fiber cannot be used as energy, but it is needed for healthy digestion. Whole grains, vegetables, fruits, and legumes (peas, beans, and lentils) all contain fiber.

All Carbohydrates Are Not Created Equal

Simple carbohydrates are found in fruit as well as in syrups, honey, and white sugar. Complex carbohydrates are found in most grain products, vegetables, and potatoes. Refined carbohydrates have had their fiber and nutrients removed. Unrefined carbohydrates still contain their fiber and nutrients.

Simple and refined carbohydrates are sources of quick energy because they easily convert to glucose and quickly enter the bloodstream. Eating large amounts of simple and refined carbohydrates may lead to health problems, such as obesity.

Complex, unrefined carbohydrates provide energy over a longer period of time. This is because the body has to work harder to convert them into glucose.

Examples of healthier carbohydrates

- Unrefined simple carbohydrates: fresh fruit
- Unrefined complex carbohydrates: oatmeal, brown rice, other whole grains, yams, vegetables

Examples of less healthy carbohydrates

- Refined simple carbohydrates: white sugar used in many baked goods and sweetened beverages
- Refined complex carbohydrates: white rice and white flour products, such as white bread, most pasta, and cookies

Vitamins and minerals are needed for many important processes in the body. These nutrients come from plants and animal-based foods.

Water makes up 50 to 65 percent of an adult's body. The human body can survive only a few days without taking in water. Water is necessary for nearly every chemical reaction and process within the body.

To form a daily eating plan, you can start with a guide that recommends numbers of servings of different food groups. The U.S. Department of Agriculture has developed a visual guide for daily eating called MyPyramid. MyPyramid uses bands of different colors to represent the five major food groups plus fats and oils. A healthy diet includes foods from each group every day. On the left side of the pyramid, the figure climbing the steps is a reminder to stay active.

Staying Well

Many books and websites can help you learn more about good nutrition and how to take care of your body. The tips below can all be part of your wellness tool kit.

- A healthy food plan includes a balance of nutrients. This balance should take into account your gender, age, and level of physical activity. Check food labels so that you know what you are eating.
- Use the "Recommended Daily Calorie Intake" chart to find out how many calories you need per day. Combine this

Recommended Daily Calorie Intake for a Moderately Active Individual

Gender	Age (in years)	Daily Calorie Intake
Child	2–3	1,000–1,400
Female	4–8	1,400–1,600
	9–13	1,600–2,000
	14–18	2,000
	19–30	2,000–2,200
	31–50	2,000
	51+	1,800
Male	4–8	1,400–1,600
	9–13	1,800–2,200
	14–18	2,400–2,800
	19–30	2,600–2,800
	31–50	2,400–2,600
	51+	2,200–2,400

You may need more or fewer calories than the amount shown in this chart depending on your height and how active you are.

Source: Adapted from U.S. Department of Health and Human Services, U.S. Department of Agriculture, *Dietary Guidelines for Americans 2005*

information with MyPyramid and a balance of nutrients to create a healthy food plan.

- Pay attention to **portion** sizes. You can eat larger amounts of low-calorie foods, such as green vegetables. Eat foods that are higher in calories in smaller amounts.

- Include some treats in your healthy food plan. Some dietitians and doctors advise using an 80/20 plan. Eat healthy foods 80 percent of the time. The other 20 percent of the time, you may eat less healthful foods—in reasonable amounts.

- Eat a healthy breakfast to help you better concentrate and keep you from feeling hungry all day. A healthy breakfast includes nutritious protein and a *complex, unrefined* carbohydrate, such as oatmeal or a whole-grain cereal.

- Talk to a health professional about a healthy body weight for your height and bone structure.

- Remember that the body needs some stores of fat to be healthy. Your body mass index (BMI) measures how much of your weight is body fat. You can check your BMI to see if it falls within a healthy range for teens of your height, age, and gender. You can use an online BMI calculator, such as the KidsHealth BMI calculator at kidshealth.org.

- Consider how caffeine, artificial sweeteners, and carbonated drinks affect your body. Some people try to reduce calorie intake by drinking coffee or sodas with caffeine instead of eating. However, replacing food with caffeine is not good for the body.

You will eat every day for the rest of your life. You can protect your health by eating and exercising wisely and paying attention to your thoughts and emotions. Make healthy choices about the company you keep and how much you let social and cultural messages affect you. Caring for yourself will help you live a healthy, satisfying life.

Glossary

adolescents: Teenagers.

anxiety: A constant feeling of fear about what might happen.

binging: Eating unusually large amounts of food at one time.

blood clotting: The process by which blood changes from a liquid to a solid and stops flowing. Clotting stops the loss of too much blood.

calories: Units of measurement for energy in food.

cartilage: A strong, flexible tissue found in the joints, the outer ear, and other places in the body.

compulsively: Acting as a response to a powerful desire.

converted: Changed.

depression: A mental condition that involves long-lasting sadness and hopelessness and a lack of activity.

diagnosed: Identified as having a disease.

fast: Stop eating.

glucose: A simple sugar that the body uses for energy. Different carbohydrates are broken down into glucose quickly or slowly.

gorges: Eats an unusually large amount of food at one time.

ideals: Ideas about, or images of, what is perfect.

inherited: Received from parents, grandparents, or ancestors.

malnutrition: A serious health condition caused by lack of food, lack of certain nutrients, or inability to use nutrients taken in.

nutritional: Related to substances needed by the body for energy and tissue building.

obese: Weighing considerably more than recommended for one's height and age; having a body mass index (BMI) over 30 as an adult.

obsessed: Unable to stop thinking about something.

overwhelming: Too much to cope with.

portion: A serving of food for one person.

professional: Performed by a person who has been educated and usually has a license to do something that requires lots of skill. Doctors, nurses, and lawyers are examples of professionals.

psychological: Having to do with the mind or emotions.

psychotherapy: The nonmedical treatment of emotional and mental problems, usually through talking.

puberty: The period in life when a person's body changes from that of a child to that of an adult.

purges: Causes the body to get rid of food that was eaten, such as by forced vomiting.

relapses: The worsening of a condition after a period of improvement.

self-image: How a person judges his or her own worth.

urge: A strong desire.

willpower: The power to make a decision and follow through with it.

Find Out More

Books

Bickerstaff, Linda. *Nutrition Sense: Counting Calories, Figuring Out Fats, and Eating Balanced Meals.* New York: Rosen Publishing Group, 2009.

Favor, Lesli J. *Food as Foe: Nutrition and Eating Disorders.* New York: Marshall Cavendish, 2008.

Heller, Tania. *Eating Disorders: A Handbook for Teens, Families, and Teachers.* Jefferson, NC: McFarland and Co., 2003.

Lawton, Sandra Augustyn, editor. *Eating Disorders Information for Teens: Health Tips About Anorexia, Bulimia, Binge Eating, and Other Eating Disorders.* Detroit: Omnigraphics, 2005.

Websites

Anorexia Nervosa and Related Eating Disorders, Inc.
http://www.anred.com

Centers for Disease Control and Prevention
http://www.cdc.gov/HealthyLiving/

MyPyramid
http://www.mypyramid.gov

National Eating Disorders Association
http://www.nationaleatingdisorders.org

TeensHealth (Nemours Foundation)
http://www.kidshealth.org/teen

Index

Page numbers for photographs and illustrations are in **boldface**.